BIRTHDAY FARTS

JANE BEXLEY

ISBN 9798375668352

Hip, hip, hooray! It's the best time of year!
My birthday is coming and soon will be here.
We'll plan the best party and pick the best theme.
It will be crazy and fun and have cake and ice cream.

"How about bowling," mom asks,
"or pirates or space?"
But none of those themes put a
smile on my face.

"What about swimming or robots? Ninjas or Mickey?"
But those aren't right either. Wow, this is tricky!

I want something unique;
something special to me.

Something that hasn't
been done throughout all
history.

I try thinking deep, digging
down to my roots.
"I've got it!" I shout. "My theme
will be...

TOOTS!

Mom and dad are stunned silent (by my brilliance no doubt).
They just sit there and stare while I plan it all out.

We'll need gas-powered snacks like broccoli and cheese, prune juice and cabbage and all kinds of beans. Of course we'll have ice cream and birthday cake too, But fart-growing foods will be best for my crew.

Once my guests have all eaten and we're ready to burst, we'll play party games and see who pops first.

Musical chairs is how we will start,
but we'll add whoopie cushions for guaranteed farts.

After running in circles our legs will be tired,
so we'll play some fart bingo (no leg work required).

Pin the Toot on the Donkey will be the next round.
We can use our toot power to spin us around.
We'll dizzily stick paper farts on the wall,
and try not to gag on the smell when we fall.

We'll go on a hunt, but not for treasure or toys.
My buddies will search for the biggest fart noise!

Duck, Duck, Toots is the last game we will play.
We'll toot on our friends then run quickly away!

After five farty games we'll be ready to stop,
so we'll gather together and sit with a plop.
I'll open my presents of all shapes and sizes
and give bags of toot loot with candy and prizes.

When the food and the games and the gifts are all done,
Mom will bring out the cake for our last bit of fun.

They'll sing happy birthday to the tune we all know while I take a deep breath for one big final...

...BLOW!

"Look," says dad, "I love a good tooty blast,
but this party might have a bit too much gas.
Why don't we try out a different theme?
Let's finish our lunch while we think as a team."

But my wheels have already started to spin
and I have an idea that triggers a grin.
"I've got it!" I say between gulps and slurps.
"I think that my party's new theme should be..."

BURPS!

Made in United States
Orlando, FL
30 November 2024

54717191R00022